Ducks on Trucks

Written by Samantha Montgomerie

Illustrated by Andy Rowland

Collins

Splash Pond is little. The ducks must cram in.

"We need room to swim and splash," yells Splish.

Quack has a plan. He needs the gang to help.

The gang looks at the plan.

Beep! The ducks in trucks bump along the track.

Quack grins. He shifts rocks and dumps them.

Diggers dig clumps of mud.
They shift sand.

The ducks thump nails with
big hammers.

thump

Ducks jump and flip. They drop and flop.

Ducks spin and crash. They bump and bash.

Ducks swish and spin. They drop and splash.

Quack sips and grins.

Splash pond

15

Letters and Sounds: Phase 4

Word count: 100

Focus on adjacent consonants with short vowel phonemes, e.g. *splash*

Common exception words: little, he, the, we, to, of, they

Curriculum links: Understanding the world

Curriculum links (National Curriculum, Year 1): Science: Animals, including humans

Early learning goals: Reading: read and understand simple sentences; use phonic knowledge to decode regular words and read them aloud accurately; read some common irregular words; demonstrate understanding when talking with others about what they have read

National Curriculum learning objectives: Reading/word reading: read accurately by blending sounds in unfamiliar words containing GPCs that have been taught; Reading/comprehension: understand both the books they can already read accurately and fluently and those they listen to by checking that the text makes sense to them as they read, and correcting inaccurate reading

Developing fluency

- Encourage your child to follow the words as you read the first pages with expression.
- Take turns to read a page, encouraging your child to read the spoken words and speech bubbles in a voice that matches the characters.

Phonic practice

- Practise reading words that contain adjacent consonants. Encourage your child to sound out and blend the following:

  crash   trucks   clumps   flop

- Challenge your child to sound out the following words. Can they match the word with a word above that rhymes?

  drop   dumps   ducks   splash

Extending vocabulary

- Focus on words that sound like the things they describe. Can your child think of similar sound words?

  splash (e.g. *splosh, splish*)   bash (e.g. *thump, bong*)   beep (e.g. *ting, ding*)